I See A Smile

Written By LaTasha Reinhardt
Illustrated By Emily Hercock

D1607249

Copyright © 2022 by LaTasha Reinhardt

All rights reserved. No part of this publication may be reproduced, distributed or transmitted in any form or by any means, including photocopying, recording, or other electronic or mechanical methods, without the prior written permission of the publisher, except in the case of brief quotations embodied in critical reviews and certain other noncommercial uses permitted by copyright law.

Scripture quotations taken from The Holy Bible, New International Version® NIV® Copyright © 1973 1978 1984 2011 by Biblica, Inc. ™ Used by permission. All rights reserved worldwide.

Dedication

———◆———

This book is dedicated to every family with a baby on the way with a cleft lip, cleft palate, or both.

The news may feel like it is too much to bear right now, but soon your sweet baby will be in your arms and all your fears will melt away. Your baby is perfect just the way they are—God does not make mistakes.

"For I know the plans I have for you," declares the Lord, "plans to prosper you and not to harm you, plans to give you hope and a future."

Jeremiah 29:11 NIV

———◆———

This Book Belongs To

Acknowledgments

❦

I must start by thanking **God** for putting this amazing dream in my heart and directing my path through to its completion. Never in a million years would I have dreamed of writing a children's book, but here I am!

Next, thank you to my husband, **Nate**. From listening to my endless conversations about writing a book, reading my first drafts, and offering unconditional support—I could not have done this without you. Thank you so much, my love.

I should also mention my sweet boys, who were the inspiration for this story.

Theo, thank you for showing me that in our purest form we don't see differences, we just see smiles.

Asher, you are the strongest, happiest little boy in this world. Thank you for filling our family with so much joy and brightening the world with your smile.

When my brother was still in my Mommy's belly she told me that the baby would look different when he was born.

She told me it was called a cleft lip and that it didn't hurt him, but that his smile would look different from mine.

We spent a lot of time waiting for him to come—I even got to help get his room ready!

Daddy said I was going to be the best big brother.

The day my brother finally came home from the hospital with Mommy and Daddy, I was so excited to meet him!

But I was nervous too because I didn't know how he would look.

When I peeked over the blanket and looked down at his face, I wasn't nervous anymore.

I saw my brother, and he looked perfect to me!

When the world looked at my brother
they saw a cleft...I saw a smile.

He had to go to lots of doctor's appointments, and they put tape over his lip that covered a lot of his face.

I got to be a good helper and hold his hand whenever Mommy and Daddy changed his tape!

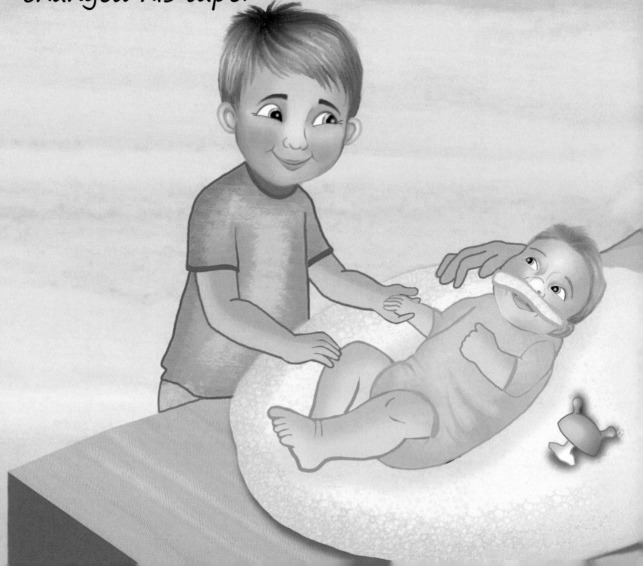

When the world saw my brother they saw the tape...I saw a smile.

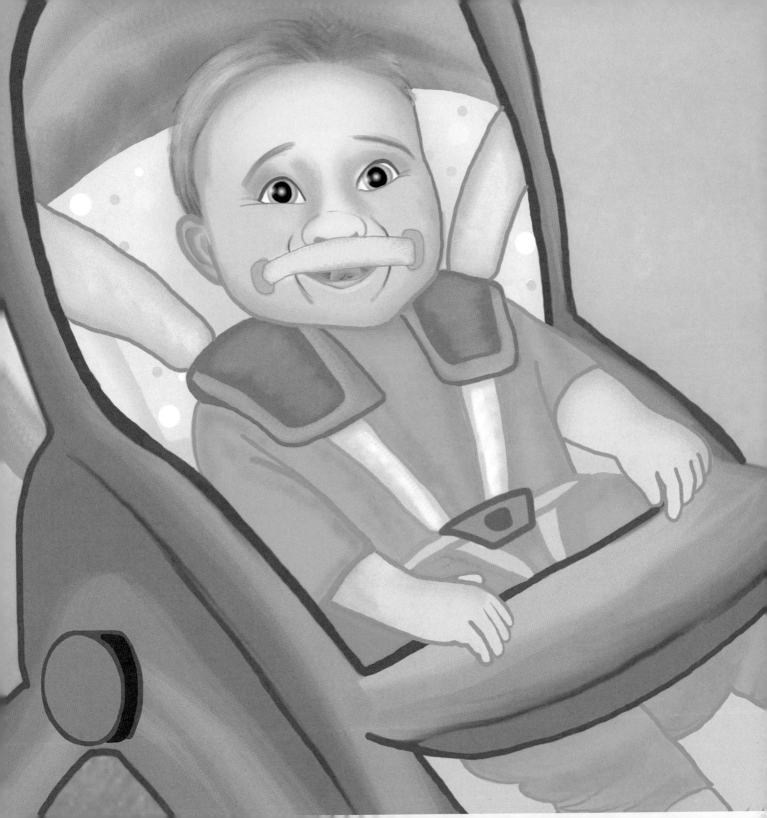

He had to go to the hospital to have surgery to bring his lip together. Mommy and Daddy said he was getting his forever smile!

He stayed overnight at the hospital with Mommy and Daddy, and I got to stay with Grandma and Grandpa!

He came home the next day, and I was so excited to see him!

I was worried that he was hurt because he had to wear arm immobilizers on his arms.

Mommy and Daddy told me that they didn't hurt him—they were to keep him from touching his lip while it healed.

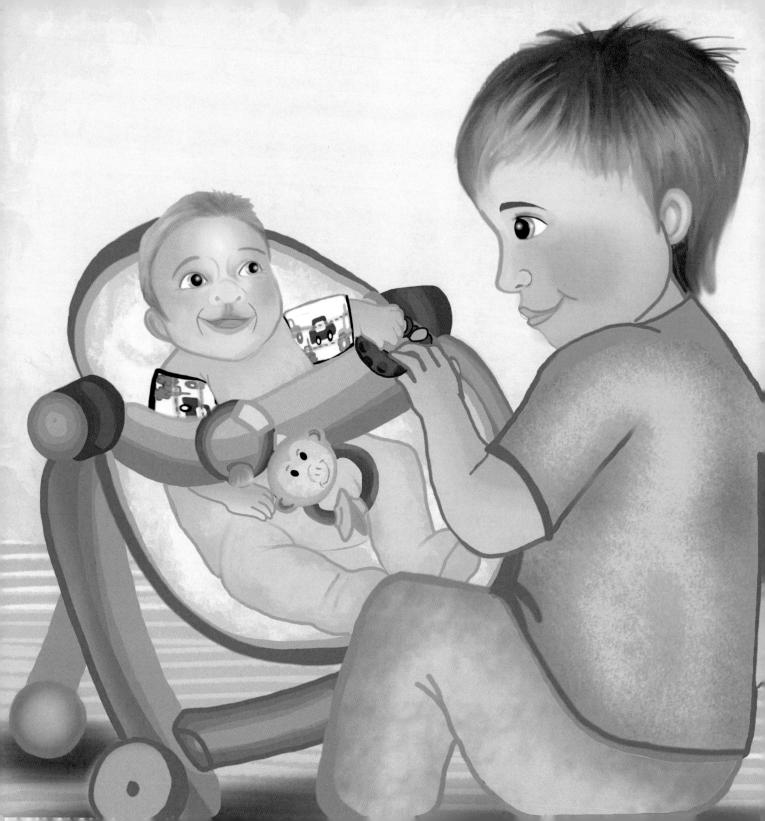

While he had to wear his arm immobilizers, I got to be a good helper and give him toys when he couldn't reach them.

After two weeks they were removed, and he could play with me again!

When the world looks at my brother they see a scar...

I see a smile.

Made in the USA
Monee, IL
29 September 2022

14931798R00017